Purposefully Broken

Discovering Your Purpose in The Brokenness of Your Past

By:
Nicole R. Dudley

Dedication

Purposefully Broken is dedicated to every woman who has been broken by the hardships and trials of life. For those who feel as if their past hinders them from discovering their God given purpose. Sis I was Purposefully Broken to help you heal. My obedience is for your deliverance.

ISBN: 978-1-9485813-4-9

www.brdpublications.com

"To everything there is a season, and a purpose under the heaven: A time to be born, and a time to die; a time to plant, and a time to pluck up that which is planted; A time to kill, and a time to heal; a time to break down, and a time to build up; A time to weep, and a time to laugh; a time to mourn, and a time to dance; A time to cast away stones, and a time to gather stones together; a time to embrace, and a time to refrain from embracing; a time to get, and a time to lose; a time to keep, and a time to cast away; A time to rend, and a time to sew; a time to keep silent, and a time to speak; A time to love, and a time to hate; a time of war, and a time of peace"

Ecclesiastes 3:1-8 (KJV)

Table of Contents

Introduction

Writing this book was birthed out of a roller coaster of an experience I had this year. In November 2017, it snowed in the south. Where I'm from snow is not common. One day I noticed I had a runny nose, but I figured it was the beginnings of a cold. Little did I know it was not a cold at all. It was Cerebrospinal fluid (CSF) leaking from my nose.

In August 2018, I finally went to the doctor, and was diagnosed with the CSF leak. The leak happened because of the increased pressure on my brain, which caused cracks in the layers of tissue between my skull and brain. When the doctor came in the room to tell me the news, I knew something was wrong because of the look on his face. This doctor was my family's (ENT) Ear, Noise, and Throat doctor. He performed several of my family member's surgeries, including my dad and nephew; but my case was beyond his scope of expertise. He took me by the hand and told me he wanted to refer me to a doctor in another town who specialized in this type of surgery. He assured me on my surgery day he would come to be with me for support. After he left the room I sat speechless, and in awe of the news. Immediately, I heard the Holy Spirit say, "Worship me." I began to worship the Lord and thanking him in advance for my healing. My surgery was on September 4, 2018, a day I will never forget.

While I was home recovering for six weeks, God began taking me through yet another purging process. My faith was truly being tested. I battled with loneliness due to being on bed rest. I grudgingly called this season of my life 'house arrest.' I realized God was teaching me to put my trust in Him and not man. I was hit with so many obstacles, but the Lord saw me through each one.

Every morning I would sit up in bed and tell the Lord I did not understand, but I trusted him. Honestly, I continued to question God concerning why I was going through this storm at this point in my life. In John 9:1-3, Jesus healed a man who was blind from birth and His disciples asked, "Lord who sinned?" Jesus answered and said, "Neither man sinned, nor his parents: but that the works of God should be made manifest in him." Gods glory was made manifest in my brokenness. During those six weeks I was home recovering the Lord revealed to me it was time to share my story with the world.

Once the Lord placed it in my heart to tell my story, He also revealed the urgency and need for my testimony to be shared with others. "Purposefully Broken," is for all women who have struggled with insecurities, self-esteem, abandonment, and identity issues. This is your time of freedom. I was sent on divine assignment to inspire you to lean on Christ, our solid rock. I struggled with not knowing who I was. I often looked at other Christian women and felt I was unable to fulfill the mandate of God on my life because of all the wrong I had done. For years I thought so little of myself, as a result I latched on to men for validation and identity.

God took this broken, dirty, filthy misshapen lump of clay and turned me into a fearfully and wonderfully made woman for Christ. God revealed to me He anointed and called me to preach His Word in order to spread the Gospel of Jesus Christ. During this time God also revealed to me He would use my past as part of my ministry. A true testament to the statement Broken crayons still color.

Once I began writing my book, the enemy immediately attempted to silence me through putting doubt in my mind. Whispering suggestions, like; "No one cares about your past. How do you expect of publish your book? Seriously, you are going to let the whole world know how low down you were?" Subsequently, my answer to the enemy was YES. Yes, I am going to share my story because it is what the Lord told me to do.

I am compelled to share my story to encourage women all over the world. Purposefully Broken is a message to all women young and old. It simply echoes no matter how bad you think you have messed up, or how low down you think you might be. The Lord will turn all of your heartaches and mistakes around for His good. One of my favorite scriptures is Romans 8:28 (KJV) 'And we know that all things work together for the good of them that love God, to them who are called according to his purpose.' This scripture led me to my title, Purposefully Broken. It was through the brokenness of my past God affirmed my true purpose. In times past, I have watched how God would use my life for his glory, and I am currently in expectation for what is to come. Honestly, without my past I would not be able to share my story or my future with you. Look out world here comes Nicole R. Dudley.

*My number one goal in life is to do God's will. I want to do what He has called, chosen, and qualified me to do. As I began to write, I was unsure of how much of my past I should include. I believe if God chooses to use you, he uses all of you. Let me take you on my journey of how I discovered my God given purpose through my broken past. Just a heads up, the names in the book were changed to protect the privacy of those involved. I truly give God al the glory for the things he has done.

------ Nicole R. Dudley

Chapter One

Innocence

I never really experienced a normal childhood. Growing up in a two parent Christian home with four sisters in a nice part of town to many seems quite normal. For me, nothing was normal about it. I was introduced to sex at an early age. I honestly do not remember how old I was when I first saw or had my first encounter with sex. I do however remember my cousins bringing guys into my grandmother's house. I watched as a line of guys waited in the backyard to have sex with my cousins. My grandmother would have some of her friends over, and she would be in the living room entertaining completely unaware of what was taking place in her house. I can recall standing there wondering if my cousins would get caught. This was a normal part of my life. On Friday nights, my sisters and I would beg and plead with my parents to let us stay with my grandmother. We affectionally called "Mo Mo." She lived in the hood, the ghetto. There was always something going on in the hood: men going to jail, women getting beat by their boyfriends, and so on.

As I stated earlier, I do not remember how old I was when I first encountered sex; but I do remember the first time I was touched. One Friday, I slept over at my grandmother's house. My cousins lived with my grandmother. When people think of molestation they often think of the opposite sex. Well, this was not the case for me. My molesters were females, and they were sisters. During this time, they were teenagers between the ages of fourteen and sixteen. We did not have the luxury of our own beds. We had to sleep with my cousins or my grandmother. I can remember vividly one night I slept with my cousin because we were up late watching movies. I refused to watch another episode of "Mommas Family" with my grandmother. My cousins and I were not close, but they were fun to be around. We played prank phone calls in the middle of the night. My favorite call to make was to ask someone if their refrigerator was running. If they said yes, we would tell them to go catch it. One night while in the bed with one of my cousins, she asked me to touch her private area. I did not know how to feel or react. I still remember how my body felt during this time. Whew, this was something totally new for me. We continued to have sex with one another for a period of three years. Sad to say, but true this was my life on Friday nights. I felt so ashamed because in my mind I knew this was wrong, but my body reacted to it. Honestly, I did the only thing I knew how to do, and that was to bury my feelings. As I buried my feelings, I also allowed hatred to grow and manifest itself in my heart. I hated my cousins, both of them. They never gave me a chance to be a kid and experience innocence.

Although I tried burying my feelings, it did not work. I can remember sitting at home watching music videos with my sisters. While watching the videos I recall seeing half naked women in bikinis shaking their bodies. The entire time I watched, I became aroused. During family outings when I saw women dressed up all fancy. Without warning, my body would go crazy. I was a preteen experiencing all these different emotions with no one to talk to about it. I could not tell my parents because they would no longer allow me to visit my grandmother's house. I loved my Mo Mo dearly, so I kept quiet. Eventually, I began to feel guilty because my body craved the feeling, but my mind wanted no parts of it. Confusion set in, and I could no longer comprehend how I truly felt about what was happening. Finally, I decided the best thing to do was to convince myself I did not like women. How does a preteen convince herself she did not like women you might ask? Simple, I diverted all of my attention to liking the opposite sex.

Chapter Two

Who Am I????

On April 28, 2001, my life changed yet again. It was the day after my 13th birthday. My parents allowed me to sleep over for the night at one of my friend's house the day before. She lived on the other side of town, so I was excited to go. We stayed up late laughing and talking about boys. My friend was already having sex with guys. She shared with me how painful it was, but how good it felt. Unknown to her, my only sexual experiences had been with girls. As she shared her stories with me, I became terrified. Finally, we called it a night, but the thoughts were still running through my mind. On Saturday afternoon while sitting on her mom's porch, we picked up with our conversation from the previous night. My friend made a joke, but I took her seriously. She said, "Nicole, the first guy who talks to you today, you must have sex with him." Now my friend was considered to be shapely by boys. On the other hand, I had no shape at all. Guys did not approach me, so I accepted her challenge. Boy was I in for a rude awakening.

Later that afternoon, we saw a man driving down the street and asked him to take us back to my side of town. One of the guys my friend was involved with lived a few blocks from my house., He wanted to see her, so we hitched a ride with the man. During the entire ride I began to regret the decision I made earlier that day. One we arrived at her boyfriend's house there were so many people. I decided to wait outside for them to finish their business. Eventually, I walked down the street and sat down on the steps of an abandoned house. As I sat lost in thought, I looked up and saw a guy walking down the street. Immediately, I became nervous and asked God please do not allow this guy to speak to me. Truly, I was not ready to honor our bet. As the guy came closer I was becoming even more nervous... Guess what? He spoke to me! Not only did he speak to me, but he walked up and introduced himself.

I do not know why to this day, but I told him about the bet. He was much older than me. He was in his mid-20's, and my thirteenth birthday was the day prior. When I explained to him about the bet. All of a sudden, he ripped off his shirt, broke the window, and unlock the door. At this point, I was afraid to turn back. Everything within me desired to know the truth about my sexual identity. I desperately wanted to know if I was attracted to men or women.

Growing up in church, I knew deep in my heart it was wrong to be with the same sex. Daily I battled within myself, I was too young to understand all of this. I never imagined myself grappling with these decisions at such a tender age. For me, this was the most painful experience I ever had. Once I made it home I had to pretend I was ok. Living in a house with eight people made it easy to hide my true feelings.

We moved in with my grandmother to take care of her, because her health was failing. My grandmother, uncle, parents, four sisters, along with myself lived in a four-bedroom home. Do not forget about our pets, two birds and a dog. Due to my grandmother needing constant care, it was easy to slip in and out of the house without being noticed. Although my first sexual encounter with a man was painful, it aroused something in me being with a female did not do and the spiral began...

Chapter Three

Someone, Anyone, Please Help Me!!!!!!!!!!

Losing and regaining your identity can be a fight. On the inside, I was still trying to discover who I was. I never saw the guy who broke my virginity again. Every night I would lay in bed with thoughts racing through my mind as I tried to sleep. The urge to hook up with the man I met while sitting on the doorstep came often. I desired to experienced what happened in that moment again.

About a week later, I learned the first man I gave myself to was murdered at a local pool hall over 50 cents. My life seemed to take a downward turn, before it even had a real chance to begin. For the next five years, I threw myself into having sex with men. The question of who I was did not bother me anymore. Sadly, I discovered I not only enjoyed sex, but I loved it. I did not realize at that time that those men were simply taking advantage of me, and I was taking advantage of them. Day after day, week after week, I was giving my body away to someone somewhere. At this point I know you may be wondering where my parents were during all of this folly. My answer to you is, they were home taking care of my elderly grandmother and my uncle.

From the very beginning, I never thought I was pretty. No one knew it, but I hated mirrors. I became good at pretending. I became a pro at the game. I was not a bad kid. I was just sneaky, so I used that to my advantage. After school, I would go to a friend's house to "play." I never went where my parents told me I could go. I would sneak off to a totally different location. Even though both my parents were in the home and raised us to know the Lord, I still felt unloved. No one saw how messed up my life had become. Consequently, because no one noticed me, I felt if men noticed me, they liked me. The mere thought of finally being accepted by someone, was refreshing.

I did not grow up thinking I was beautiful or attractive. When I looked in the mirror, everything about me was wrong. I remember looking in the mirror thinking I was fat. Therefore, I began to make myself vomit after I ate. My family assumed I was in the bathroom because I had to go. The ugly truth was I began putting my finger down my throat, and my confidence was in sex.

One might say I had two different personalities. When I was not having sex, or around my friends and family. I was a shy, timid, young girl. Being with different guys made me feel confident and outspoken. Once my parents discovered I was having sex it was all over for me. You already know my but was torn out the frame. However, no one was truly concerned why I turned to sex at the age of 13. I remained quiet because I felt no one truly cared. They were not interested in the issues which led me to this point.

Chapter Four

He Kept Me in The Midst of It All

I was in my senior year of high school, and those feeling of wanting to be with a female started to resurface. My old obsession of watching girls again and getting aroused was back. One evening, one of my friends from school came over to hangout. As we were watching a movie in my room. She began to tell me she liked girls. I was afraid to admit to her I thought I did too. Due to fear of the unknown I remained quiet when she told me. A few weeks later I found myself being intimate with my friend. Afterwards, I felt so ashamed. I knew this was not normal, so I prayed to the Lord to take away the desire to be with the same sex. I am so thankful and grateful God heard my cry. From that moment forward, I no longer desired being intimate with the same sex.

Growing up, I never had a relationship with God. I always prayed before I went to bed because my parents instilled it in us. Upon graduating from high school, I received my first bible from our church as a gift. As I reflect on my childhood in church I was taught religion. Once deliverance took place in my life, I was introduced to a relationship with Christ.

In 2007, I do not remember how, but my parents found out my cousins had molested me all those years ago. Immediately, I thought to myself. Finally, they are going to ask me if I was ok and console me. Instead, my parents swept it under the rug. No one mentioned a word about it.

Three years later, my dad officiated the wedding of one of my cousins who molested me. I tried everything in my power to get out of it, but I was forced to go. For years, I held hatred in my heart. I wondered how my life would be different if I was never touched as a child. At this point, I felt so alone because the secret I had been holding onto for years. The very reason I remained isolated and closed off, was out and no one did anything about it. I still remember the day my dad found out I was sexually active. The words he spoke still ring loudly in my ear even now. Every time I left the house he would say, "You are going to whore around in those streets!' "You are out there giving your body to every Tom, Dick, and Harry." "So, you are out there being a slut." Honestly, it hurt me to hear him say those words. Mainly, because no one ever stopped to say, "Nicole I am here for you, I love you," or, "What is going on?"

The summer after high school, I hooked up with a guy named Travis, but everyone called him TJ. He was in prison on attempted murder charges and had to wear an ankle monitor. I found myself falling head over hills for him. For some odd reason I was attracted to thugs and drug dealers. I told my parents about T.J., but of course they did not agree with me seeing him.

Early one morning, he called to tell me he wanted to be with me, but not as long as I was living with my parents. Later that day, my dad was scolding me about something I did not do. I "talked" back to him, and he slapped me across the face. The back of my earring scratched my face, and it started to bleed. Things were pretty intense in my house by this point. I called my best friend, and she asked her parents if I could come to stay with them. They agreed! I could no longer take being called a slut any longer.

Shortly after moving with my friend, TJ of course threw me to the side. He wanted nothing to do with me anymore. Within days he was back in prison because he violated his parole. Therefore, he had to serve the remaining years of his sentence. I was hurt due to the fact he had to go away, but I was familiar with being hurt. Many times, I knew I deserved better.

God began dealing with me when I moved in with my best friend and her family. I was tired, but not physically. My position of being tired was directly linked to sleeping around with different people. I wanted better! In my heart I truly believed I deserved better. I began attending weekly bible studies with my friend at her church. I watched and listened intently as her pastor and his wife taught bible study. It truly amazed me how they knew so much about the Lord. Before I knew it, I raised my hand and told them I desire to know God in this manner. I wanted a relationship with Christ.

I felt something drawing me closer. Soon I realized it was the Holy Spirit. I started seeking and wanting to know more about God's love. I grew up in church all my life, but I did not really know God. I looked forward to attending weekly bible studies and Sunday service. As I look back, this was the first sign, or shift towards my purpose. Every step I took, God was present. He did not allow me to move in with just anyone. My best friend's' parents were saved, Holy Ghost-filled believers. The Lord prepared their hearts to have me come and live with them. In the midst of it all, He was keeping me; and I did not realize it.

Chapter Five

Moving Forward

One Sunday morning while attending worship service, I noticed the guy on the drums. Let me tell you… I thought he was so handsome. After service, I asked my best friend about him. He was the pastor's youngest son. Next, I asked her for his name and she told it was Calvin. I began crushing on him in that very moment. As I stated before, my heart was seeking the Lord, but the broken little girl on the inside of me was secretly desiring the pastor's son. All jokes aside I never acted on anything with Calvin. He was a childhood crush.

Oddly, every Sunday after that encounter, I felt something strange happening to me. Living in sin was becoming tiresome and old. The thrill I felt from sleeping with men was fading away. The reason I call what I was experience strange, is because it was totally new for me. The feeling became so strong. It was literally overtaking me, and I had to share it with my friends. One day I came to the realization it was time for me to surrender my life to Christ.

After service one Sunday, an announcement was made in regard to the pastor's wife preaching in a neighboring city. My friends' parents, my bestie, and I traveled to the church to support her. The message she ministered still leaps in my spirit. It was centered around letting go of the old man and allowing God to make you new. As the sermon was being preached, I began to cry. A heaviness came upon me so strong, I felt the urge to release. Once the sermon was over, an invitation was extended to come to the altar. The pastor stated if there is anyone who desires to be saved, come now for prayer. Before I could wrap my mind around stepping out, my feet were in motion walking down the aisle.

As I lifted up my hands, the pastor's wife asked me if I believed Jesus died for my sins and rose on the third day with all power in his hands. My answer was "Yes!" Once we made it home I called my parents and asked if I could come back home. I felt like the prodigal son who took all his possessions and left home. Only to come to himself and return to find his father waiting for him with open arms. The night I returned home, my mom was frying fish. She did not yell or fuss at me. She simply fixed me a plate of food to eat, and we sat down as a family at the table. Every since this day, fish has become my absolute favorite food.

Chapter Six

Another Chance

The day I stood at the altar and gave my life to Jesus was my first personal encounter with God. Once I returned home, my determination was to get my life right. A few weeks later I began to accomplish some major goals in my life. I acquired my driver's license and enrolled in the pharmacy technician program at a local community college.

Little did I know, God was directing me to my purpose. Prior to this point I had no real interest in becoming a pharmacy technician. Honestly, I simply wanted more for myself. I took the entrance exam and passed it on the first try. Once I entered the program, my passion for pharmacy began to emerge. Upon graduating from the program, I was offered a job at a local pharmacy in my area. Finally, I reached a point in my life where everything was working in my favor. I had a license, a car, and a career. I was alone for the first time in years; not because I wanted to be, but because I had no one to sleep with.

For the next three years everything was fine, so I thought. Each year, I celebrated my celibacy. During this time, I did not truly seek the Lord, or attempt to read my bible. Honestly, I believed everything was working in my favor. Until one night while out with my two best friends. We decided to attend a bonfire to meet up with some guys. Imagine your girls bringing you somewhere, because they do not want you to be alone. Before I knew it one of my friends called her boyfriend to bring one of his boys meet us. Here we go again! This guy was so fine from the top of his head, to the soles of his feet. George was about 6'6 very stocky, a cornbread-feed man. We hit it off that night on so many levels. George and I shared numerous commonalities.

Our parents knew each other quite well. We were both the fourth of five siblings. He was a nice church going guy who loved the Lord. George was looking for a wife. With all my heart I tried to be what he desired. In the beginning, I believed I could possibly be his wife. However, those thoughts I had years before came flooding back.

Chapter Seven

Emotional Roller-coaster

Every time I was around George my body yearned to be intimate with him. We were in two separate places because he did not desire sex from me. Due to his continual denying me, feelings of rejection began to set in. My mindset led me to believe if I could get a guy to want me, I would feel validated and accepted. George was different. He wanted to get to know me, which was unfamiliar to me. I pressured him so much he finally gave into my yearnings.

On my 20th birthday, we finally had the chance to come together. I felt like I had scored the jackpot! Total excitement does not even begin to explain my level of emotions. A major accomplishment was taking place with George. I waited patiently for this moment, and I was finally getting what I wanted. My obsession with George grew stronger each day. I called and texted him nonstop, begging him to be with me again. Each time he would ignore my calls or simply tell me no, I was not willing to accept "no!" My mind could not handle the rejection. I wrote him letters daily telling him how much I wanted to be with him. We would meet at Burger King in the parking lot quite often. He would read my letters and try his best not to hurt my feelings by letting me down. The constant rejection from George nearly broke me. This was totally foreign territory for me. Guys from my past were always eager to be with me. I believed the more eager they were, the more they wanted me.

Initially, it took some time for me to get over the hurt I felt. I was still attending church every Sunday, but I allowed my personal relationship with God to slip. Later I realized God never left me, but I walked away from Him. As time passed, I began to get over George. Eight months had passed since my last meeting with George. Emotionally, I was just dealing with it. The rejection from George was another layer of hurt added on to bury in my grave. All of us at some point, have experienced an emotional tomb where we buried our feelings. I thank God for the one Sunday He resurrected me from my tomb. It literally changed my life.

Friends are truly gems in our times of despair. My friend invited me to a women's program at her church one Sunday evening. After service was over, we gathered outside to catch up with some of the members. As we were talking with one other, Calvin, the drummer, walked up to me. He said, "Hey, I have not seen you in a while." Deep down on the inside, I was doing back flips. Marvelous I though within myself! He finally noticed me. My next move was asking my friend to give him my number. I was in total awe to hear from Calvin that night.

I was so excited to talk to him. We talked on the phone until the sun came up. As soon as any guy showed interest in me, I would fall hard for him. Calvin was no exception. He actually seemed to like me quite a bit.

The first two weeks I spent with Calvin were so refreshing. The bond was growing stronger each day between us, and I was determined to make it work. My greatest fear was being rejected again. As we continued to talk, I found out he had a girlfriend. Initially, I was heart-broken when I learned Calvin had a girlfriend. My sadness was soon replaced with joy, because he told me he was in the process of breaking up with her. We continued to talk, because I wanted it to work. Every week I would ask him if he broke up with her. He would reply by telling me he was trying to end the relationship. He would visit his ex every weekend. Supposedly, to break up with her. I continued to talk to him daily. One day I awoke to find myself madly in love with him just like I did before with George.

Calvin was not quick to be intimate with me either. Believe me; I tried. After a while, I was ok with not sleeping with him. I was just glad to be in a relationship with someone, anyone, who liked me.

Chapter Eight

Self-esteem What is That?

Life has a way of depleting you. I lacked confidence, identity, and self-esteem as a result of childhood traumas. Settling for Calvin was not the first time I sold myself short. If I can be transparent, I did not believe I was worthy of better. As a result, we only met up with one another at night in the park. He never came to meet my family, and vice-versa. During our nightly conversations I always asked the following questions. Why do you like me? What is it about me that you like? Why do you think I am pretty?" The reason I asked Calvin all these questions is because I did not see my true beauty, value, and self-worth. Validation from others had become my drug. Calvin and I remained in a relationship for ten years, on and off. This was my choice because I refused to believe Nicole was worthy of better.

During those ten years, we still met up in the park at night. I was in love with him. Whenever I saw his car pull up the butterflies filled my stomach. The opportunity for us to be intimate was non-existent due to both of us living with our parents.

Even though my love life was slow. God opened a major door which afforded me the opportunity to attend a well-respected Historically Black University, an hour from my home town. Finally, I was going back to school to become a pharmacist.

Tuition was extremely expensive coupled with living on campus. The solution was for me to live off campus and work full-time to help relieve the burden off my parents. I was a 24 year- old sophomore in college, living on my own for the first time. This was the life! My parents were not around to place limitations on my life. Initially, I lived as if I was still at home with my parents. Next, I began to venture out and found a church home in the city. I went to church, home, and school. Once Calvin was able to come to visit me, he and I became intimate with one other.

Due to my level of brokenness, we continued an on again off again relationship. It became very toxic, really fast. Eventually we found ourselves simply using each other for sex. There is an age-old adage which states, "birds of a feather flock together." I can say for myself this is certainly true. Soon I conclusion Calvin and I were attracted to each other's brokenness. Fear kept me from completely leaving him alone. I truly believed I could not get anyone better. If Calvin walked away who would want me. Honestly, I was not ready to deal with that giant. Despite the toxicity, I continued to deal with the arguments, mental abuse, and emotional abuse from Calvin. Even though I did not see value, identity, or confidence in myself, I always knew I was different. I was not like the rest of my family.

Throughout my journey towards discovering my purpose, my awareness surrounding my difference always remained with me.

Chapter Nine

Wondering in The Wilderness

The Lord never leaves us, we leave Him! Often times we stray so far from God it becomes difficult to hear from Him. While on the path to discovering my purpose, I wandered away from God. I found myself abiding in a spiritual wilderness. While Calvin and I were in one of our off seasons, I meet a guy online who lived in the city where I was attending college. Earlier, I mentioned conducting my life as if I still lived at home with my parents. Because of the level of respect, I hold for my parents, staying out late or going to the club was a no. However, Calvin occasionally came over to visit from time to time. One night, or should I say early one morning around 2:00 a.m. I was awakened to my phone vibrating on the night stand. Chris, who I met online wanted me to come over. Immediately, I informed him I had class in a few hours, 8:00 a.m. to be exact. He suggested I leave from his house and go to school from there. As soon as I hung up the phone it hit me. Girl, you no longer need permission to go anywhere. Finally, I could come and go as I pleased. Once we hung up, I got dressed, packed a bag, and headed to his house. Calvin and I never officially ended our relationship the night I went to be with the online guy. I was meeting him for the first time.

Once I made it to his house, we had unprotected sex and went straight to sleep. The next morning as I dressed for school was the first moment I realized how far away from God I had wandered. Literally, I cannot recall a time I stopped to think of what could have happened to me. Chris could have killed me the night I went to his home, because no one knew I was there.

Reality began to set in as thoughts bombarded my mind about my current situation with Chris and Calvin. The enemy had his hooks so far in me, but I was numb to it. The thrill of attention from the opposite sex had become my obsession. How could I allow myself to sink so deep into my fleshly desires?

Growing up, I remember hearing the old folks say, "Sin takes you farther than you want to go and keeps you longer than you want to stay." Well, this was my current state! I wanted out. I needed a diversion really fast. Help, I have fallen, and I don't know how to pull myself up.

One day while listening to the radio I heard an advertisement for a local church. This was the solution to help me break free from my current bondage. After attending the first service I became a member, because I was convinced this was where I needed to be. Everyone in the church greeted me with open arms. They knew I was a college student with no family in town. They became my family. On Sundays I attended both services because I joined the choir. The choir sang during both services. Everyone in the choir embraced me, including the drummer named Malcolm. I was not impressed by him because he was married, and I refused to go down that road. I considered Malcom as more of a big brother to me. Whenever I was in need, the choir would pitch in to help me, including Malcolm. The more he helped me, the more I appreciated him. Malcolm was fairly young. Whenever I had a problem I would call him for advice. Between services on Sundays, he would pull me aside and tell me to call him at a certain time to talk. In the beginning It seemed innocent, until I realized he was really flirting. Once I discovered he was being flirtatious my thoughts of him shifted. Suddenly, I began to desire him in a different way.

One day I reached out to Malcom to vent about an argument I had with Calvin. We argued because I wanted him to come over to see me, but Calvin refused. Malcom proceeded to tell me I needed a guy in my life who would treat me right. The next thing I noticed, the conversation shifted, and he began making sexual hints. Before too long the sexual side of Nicole poked her head in. The next words out of my mouth were, "Malcolm, I want to have sex with you." There was a long pause. During the pause my heart felt as if it was beating outside of my chest. Finally, I said it, and I could not take it back. Little did I know I would not be ready for the next words out of his mouth. finally, "Give me your address, and I will come by on Monday."

Once Monday came I was extremely nervous. I had never slept with a married man before in my life. In the back of my mind, I tried telling myself it was ok. Even though I was never a drinker, and I did not have any alcohol in my apartment to loosen me up. I decided to take two oxycodone tablets to calm my anxiousness. It worked! Next, I put blankets over my windows because I wanted it to be totally dark. Most of my sexual sins were done in the dark. I felt comfortable in the dark! All of a sudden there was a knock at the door, and it was him. He came inside, and the rest is history! We did exactly what he came over to do. This was our first time and last time being together. Unknown to us, we were blinded in our sin. God gave us a way of escape. He always does, but we must choose to take it. Looking back, I was too blind-to see the open door. Every Sunday after Malcom and I were together for the first time, my pastor preached on adultery.

I truly believe the Lord was giving me fair warning to stop before things got worse. A few Sundays later my pastor ministered a particular sermon on adultery which really convicted me. The tears began to flow uncontrollably from my eyes as I listened to the message. One of the choir members walked over and just held me. All I could utter out of my mouth was I am so sorry. This was the first time during my spiritual wilderness I truly felt convicted. I continued repeating I am so sorry over and over. Once I started to calm down, Malcom was staring at me from behind the glass surrounding the drums with an evil look on his face.

The following Monday, I texted Malcolm to tell him that I would not have sex with him anymore. For a while, we stopped, but It did not last long. My body yearned for the way he made me feel. I missed the excitement of sleeping with him and no one knew. Later that day I called him to let him know I wanted to be with him again. The first words out of his mouth were could I handle it, and I told him yes. We commenced to our usual escapade again. Malcom never used protection. On top of cheating on his wife, he was also being reckless. We were both playing with fire.

One day I began feeling sick, but I dismissed it and went about my business. Due to being diagnosed with Polycystic Ovarian Syndrome (PCOS) I did not have regular cycles. In order for my cycles to become regular, I needed to take birth control. Once I realized my cycle was late, I was worried. I was on birth control, but I forgot to pick up my refill from the pharmacy.

Immediately, I took a pregnancy test, and I saw a faint line on the stick. Once I made it to church on Sunday everything seemed to be fine. In between services, as everyone was eating breakfast, I became sick again. All of a sudden, I had to rush to the bathroom because I began feeling the urge to vomit. Many of the women came into the restroom to help me. Someone pulled up a chair for me to sit down, and I immediately just burst into tears. One of the ladies asked how far I was in my pregnancy. I did not know how to respond to her question. I just told her I was by myself. She asked me if I was ok, and I repeated I was by myself.

By now the news was spreading like wildfire around the church about me. Once I gained enough strength to get up, I walked to the car. When I checked my phone, I noticed Malcom had called me several times. He wanted to know what was going on with me. I mustered up enough courage to tell him I took a pregnancy test because I felt strange. Surprisingly, he was not upset and told me would call me later.

Chapter Ten

Exposed

Temporary moment of passion often results in years of pain, which was my case. Later that night, Malcom called me to talk about the issue at hand. He told me no one under any circumstance could know my baby was for him. Unfortunately, it was too late to retract the damage. Earlier I spoke with the pastor's wife, and she put the pieces together the baby was for Malcom. For a brief moment there was utter silence on the phone and all of a sudden, I heard rage in his voice. Frantically, he began yelling asking me why I exposed him. The next words out of his mouth caused me to tremble with fear. He cursed me so bad. I was every name under the sun, moon, and the earth. According to Malcolm I ruined his life! Umm, excuse me sir, but it goes both ways.

Once we hung up the phone my heart sank, the tears flowed, and I was more broken than ever. Honestly, I was devastated, and I could not imagine how I would recover. My whole world came crashing down, and all my dirty deeds were being exposed for the world to see.

During this time, I started a new job working at a hospital overnight as a pharmacy technician. While at work one night, I began having sharp cramps. I rushed to the bathroom only to find I was bleeding. The pharmacist on duty suggested I go straight to the emergency room. As I explained my situation to the nurse, she was led to conduct an ultrasound. A ton of emotions were running through my mind as I laid on the table. The nurse explained the ultrasound revealed no activity from the fetus. Truly, I cannot explain how I felt at that moment. When I thought I could not sink any lower into depression, I did.

A few days later I received a call from one of the choir members. She took care of me weeks prior to this catastrophe. She informed me the news about my pregnancy, and Malcolm being the father was spreading like wildfire throughout the church. I was afraid of being kicked out of the church for what I had done. There was nowhere for me to run or hide. Life can shift from bad to worse in a matter of moments. Many people in the church began treating me differently. I felt as if I was wearing the letter A on my chest. Some of the choir members refused to have anything to do with me. This transpired because Malcom was asked to leave the church, and the choir was left without a drummer.

In the midst of this travesty, I learned Malcom was involved with other women besides me as well. Over the years, the list of names continued to grow with mine now being added. At this point on my journey to discovering my purpose, this was the most difficult. Men abusing me emotionally and mentally was the norm in my life, but never before had my dirty deeds been exposed. There was nothing I could do to cover this up. A sweet smile was not going to make this go away. My best Sunday church outfit was not going to erase this. The biggest study bible was not going to make this disappear. When God exposes you, no one can help you. I ignored every way of escape He gave me. The Lord was protecting me from this. In short, because I did not listen to His voice, my dark deeds caught up with me.

One Friday night I met up with an old coworker. We went to dinner to catch up because I truly needed a diversion. During dinner, I received a call from someone who I had not seen or heard from in months. It was Chris, the guy I met online. I was still in a state of depression from the previous affair with Malcom, so I answered the phone. We held your usual catching up conversation. Hey, how have you been? What have you been up to? The next words out his mouth came in the form of him wanting to see me. The thought entered my mind to say no, but I went despite my better judgement.

Throughout my life, when something traumatic happened, I always looked to men for comfort. This time was no exception. Due to the recent pregnancy, I stopped at the store to pick up some condoms. I refused to go through another situation like before. Before Chris and I were intimate I asked him to wear some protection. At first, he agreed, however, in the middle our encounter he ripped off the condom. Immediately, I asked him why he did it. He simply said because he wanted to.

Angry does not even begin to explain my feeling at that moment. I kept telling him no, stop, but he would not. Therefore, I began fighting him off, but it did not work. He held me down and raped me. I laid there crying. On the inside, I felt like I deserved to be hurt. Once he was done, my body was sore from being held down and abused.

As I got dressed to leave he followed me to my car. He wanted me to take him to get something to eat. I told Chris my car was on empty. Once I unlocked my door, he jumped into the passenger seat and demanded I take him. As I started the car, he looked over to check my gas level. When Chris saw I had a full tank of gas, he began to curse uncontrollably. The entire ride for food seemed as if I was in a daze. Portions of me could not believe what happened to me.

All I wanted to do was get Chris out of my car. Finally, we got his food, and I dropped him off at his home. I was truly not ready for what happened next. He walked around to the driver's side of the car and told me he was not afraid to hurt women who crossed him. When Chris turned to walk away I immediately took off.

Chapter Eleven

Guilt and Shame

The drive home was long and hard. I cried from the time I pulled off, until I made it to my door. Words cannot begin to describe this journey I had traveled. As if the situation with Malcom was not enough. I found myself beyond rock bottom, but this was a whole new low.

The purpose of visiting Chris was to seek comfort, and it ended in me being raped. If only Chris had used the condom, none of this would have happened. Once I made it home, I sat in the bathtub crying with the water running. I scrubbed my skin until it was raw. How could I be at such a low point like this in my life. I truly believed I deserved to be hurt and abused because of all the wrong I had done in my life. It seemed as if all my dirty deeds had caught up with me.

At this point I was so devastated, I called my boss to tell her I could not come in to work. My boss wanted to know why, and I explained the entire ordeal from beginning to end. She advised me to go to our employee health office to apply for a leave of absence. The nurse who assisted me scheduled an appointment to have a rape kit done and to get physically checked out.

The doctor conducted a physical exam and sent the swabs to the lab for testing. The nurse also drew blood as well. A few days later, when the results came back I learned Chris had given me a Sexual Transmitted Disease (STD). Everything in my life was falling apart fast. I lost something, and I never had a chance to wrap my mind around what happened to me.

Everyone in the church knew I was sleeping with the drummer who was married. I was raped by a guy I barely knew. Now, the icing on the cake was I had an STD because of unprotected sex. Praise God the STD was curable. After all of the bad news, I stayed locked in my apartment for about a week. I did not want to talk to or see anyone. All I wanted to do was sit and wallow in my depression. Satan and his demons were having a field day with me, and I did nothing to stop it.

As I sat in my living room, I felt overwhelmed at the level of brokenness hoovering over my life. It's a must I take a moment and pause to thank God for bringing me out of the mess I was in. I believe our past remains to keep us humble, and to let us know we did not deliver ourselves. It was God and God alone who picked us up out of our mess and gave us another chance.

The bible reminds us in John 10:27-28 (KJV) 'My sheep hear my voice, and I know them, and they know me: And I give unto them eternal life; and they shall never perish, neither shall any man pluck them out of my hand.' God knew me before the foundation of the world. He knew every mistake I would make and every lie I would tell. God also knew I would listen to Him when He spoke because I am His sheep. God knew me, but I did not have a relationship with him.

One Friday while on my way to work, I called home to talk with my parents. Honestly, I had been avoiding them, because I did not want them to know what happened to me. I began telling my mom I was raped, and she started to cry. My dad was in the background asking my mom why she was crying. As my mom told my dad I had been raped, his response blew my mind. My dad believed I deserved to be raped because I was out whoring in the streets and sleeping around with everyone.

Again, no one asked me if I was ok, or how was I coping with the trauma that happened to me.

Chapter Twelve

Someone to Love Me

Pain will keep you on a continual cycle if you do not deal with it. The pain had become so undaunting I was led to seek help from a counselor on campus at the college. She told me I may be addicted to sex and worked with me to discover ways to cope with the issues I was facing. During our sessions she always gave me an assignment which forced me to confront my feelings and put them in the proper perspective. Although one part of me was seeking help, the other part of me was comfortable with the familiar. Consequently, I did not like the idea of giving up the control I believed I had over my life.

The weekly sessions caused me to see I was in a state of in-between spiritually. My sins were exposed, and I was still struggling with completely letting go of men. The Spirit of the Lord was tugging at my heart, but my mind was not ready to serve Him whole heartily. Little did I know it was all a part of his perfect plan.

One day, I decided to skip class and go to the movies. Skipping class became the norm for me. While I was at the movies, I met this guy name James and of course I gave him my number. A few hours later he called me, and we met up. The rest is history. I know already what you are thinking. I have been through Hades and back, but I am still sleeping with men. Well, yes, because it brought me a level of comfort. Honestly, it was all I knew in my life. Dysfunction had become the norm because I was not receiving the love I desired from my family. I was too afraid to confide in anyone, including my friends, about the turn my life had taken.

Men did not expect me to have it all together, because they were only interested in strictly sex. Nothing more, and Nothing less. However, when I would meet up with James and other men, the comfort I yearned to gain only lasted for the time we were together. Once they left, I would feel lonely and empty all over again. As a result, my depression began to grow worse.

After the situation with Malcom, a part of me began desiring a child more than anything. I remember scheduling an appointment with my gynecologist to determine if he could start me on fertility treatments. When he shared with me the price of the treatments, I was devastated. I wanted so badly to birth what I lost. My days and nights were consumed with thoughts about a child and how he or she would look. I was on a quest to become a mother. My journey did not stop because of the news from my doctor. I began researching programs available to help assist women trying to conceive. Envy and jealousy began to set in because women around me were pregnant, including one of my best friends. From my perspective it was unfair others could get pregnant, and I was struggling. I started buying ovulation test to determine when I would be most fertile. Of course, this led to more unprotected sex. Deep down inside my entire focus had shifted to simply have sex to get pregnant. In the back of my mind I thought a child would solve all of my problems.

Finally, I would have someone who to love me unconditionally, no questions asked. It panged me to see young women with children who did not love or care for them. In my opinion it seemed those who did not really want children became pregnant. People like me who wanted to conceive more than anything in the world, were barren.

After the situation with Malcom, I tried trapping every guy I slept with in order to conceive. I believed God was playing a joke on me because I became more reckless.

I never conceived a child, and I continued asking God why. I desperately needed someone, anyone, to love me!

Chapter Thirteen

Understanding Grace

Four years have passed since the situation with Malcom and the rape from Chris. My life has shifted in a new direction. I have a better job, my own space again, but nicer. Sadly, I never finished school. Due to my inability to focus I withdrew. The everyday pangs of my past life and current situation were a constant distraction.

One evening while sitting in my room watching a sermon on my phone by Sarah Jakes Roberts. I literally begin to sense in my spirit she was ministering directly to me and looking inside of my life. Although my surroundings were different, my personal life had not changed for the better. Calvin and I were still involved on some level. I know his name has not been mentioned in a while. The entire ordeal with Malcom, the rape, and Calvin were still lurking in the background of my mind. My life had been a roller coaster ride for the last nine years being in a relationship with Calvin. However, one day I made a tough decision to let everyone go except Calvin. After everything I endured with him, he still wanted to be with me. Even after all the mistakes I made, including sleeping with other men. He was angry I put his health in danger by having unprotected sex.

For weeks leading up to the day I watched the sermon by Pastor Roberts, I felt God was drawing me. Just like before, I began growing weary of the life I was currently living. Honestly, was tired of giving my body away. I wanted better. My heart desired better. Each sermon I heard during church was about God's forgiveness and his never-ending love for us.

Over the years I learned grace is God's unmerited favor and his goodness towards those who do not deserve it. Grace is not something we can earn or purchase, but it is given freely by God to those he chooses to bestow it upon. During this time, I truly began to ask God to remove Calvin from my life because I could not do it on my own. My words echoed let him go, but my heart was saying hold on. On numerous occasions I asked the Lord to remove Calvin from my life. I would often ask him to show me a sign, if Calvin was not the one for me. Immediately, Calvin would do something to completely devastate me, and my depression would set in. There was a war going on in my members. I was fighting to keep Calvin in my life and God was tugging at my heart to come closer. One day, out of the blue I received a text message from my best friend with a YouTube link to a sermon by pastor Roberts. As I watched the message I literally felt the presence of God calling me into a place of worship and prayer.

Prayer had become like a foreign language to me. I had not prayed in such a long time, and I did not know how to begin. Before I knew it, my mouth was moving, and I was telling God I was tired, and I wanted to change. Little did I know today would be the beginning of change for me. I sat on the floor in the corner of my bedroom and surrendered my life to the Lord. A song entered my heart as I sat with tears streaming down my faced entitled, 'Oh How I Love Jesus.' As I began singing this song, every burden began to lift and mistakes I made were lifting off of me. My tears began to flow uncontrollably. I still remember sitting on the floor, rubbing my hands up and down my arms as if I was shedding off the old me. A small still voice whispered in my ear, "I have called you to preach the gospel." God told me He would use my past as a part of my ministry to share my story with women all over the world. If he could do it for me, he can do it for you.

I was led by the spirit to Acts 3:6-7 (KJV), "Then Peter said, Silver and gold have I none; but such as I have given I thee: In the name of Jesus Christ of Nazareth rise up and walk. And he took him by the right hand and lifted him up: and immediately his feet and ankle bones received strength." For the first time in my life, I understood what I read in the bible. It was as if God had opened my eyes to the meaning of His Word. The Lord revealed my purpose in the midst of my brokenness, in spite of my past.

Chapter Fourteen

The Evolution of Purpose

It was the day before Thanksgiving 2017, one of my best friends and I were eating at iHop. During breakfast, I felt led to share with her about my past experiences with men. She was very supportive and caring. It was an opportunity for me to finally be transparent with her. Even though I was able to share my heart, the question still lingered in my head. Who's going to listen to me preach with all the things I have done.

Recently, I found myself replaying my experience with the Lord in the corner of my bedroom. It was still hard for me to accept God wanted to use me. After Christmas, I moved again and called Calvin to help me. He was beyond elated to help, because we were an item again. A few weeks passed before he came to visit again. One night he decided to come over for dinner. I made pasta and baked cookies for dessert. While sitting at the table I asked Calvin if he was tired of us sleeping together, and of course he said no. I told Calvin God was not pleased with our actions. We sat quietly on the sofa holding hands and watching television for a moment. Before I knew it, we were back to our usual routine. After he left, I decided to finish my leftovers from dinner, when all of a sudden, I had what I have coined my, "Damascus Experience."

Before I could place the first bite in my mouth, the Lord appeared to me. It was during that moment He showed me myself! Immediately, I fell back in the chair and my entire life flashed before me. I began to repent and cry out to the Lord. I never ate the pasta that night because I decided to fast. I wanted the Lord to know I was serious about serving Him. For the next three days I fasted, drinking only water during the day and one meal at night. My free time was spent praying and watching sermons on YouTube by Heather and Cornelius Lindsey.

During this time, God began to pour back into me. I purchased a better bible, one with large print, and I started to read. He began waking me up each morning between the hours of two and five o'clock. Once I was awake, the first thing I did was grab my bible and read.

In my new apartment, I had no furniture. There was an air mattress and a fold away chair. Early in the morning, I would sit in the chair to read for hours until my alarm sounded for work. After work, I would sit at the counter in my fold away chair and become totally engrossed in God's word. I began reading the New Testament, because I wanted to know who Jesus was for myself. My desire was to have my own encounter with Him. On Fridays, I would spend my nights with Jesus. I loved getting lost in His word. Never in my life had I read the bible in this way. A greater level of revelation and wisdom came from my commitment to serve Him. The more I read the bible, the more I realized who I had become. You never know how blind you are until Jesus removes the scales from your eyes and allows you to see.

As I began to grow closer to God, He revealed to me that in my lowest most shameful moments He never left me. When I was being molested, He was there. When I did not know if I liked men or women, He was there. When I felt unloved, He was there. When I felt I was ugly with low self-esteem, He was there. When I was exposed, He was there. God exposed and shielded me all at the same time. Malcom's wife could have found me and hurt me. The STD I had could have been incurable. God was not playing a joke on me like I believed before. He revealed to me He was protecting my womb by not allowing me to get pregnant. All those years I went through life thinking no one loved, or cared, but God showed me His unwavering love.

One Saturday, my friend called and invited me to bible study in her home. Her father-in-law was a minister and began weekly bible study for family and friends. My mind was set on attending, because I was eager to learn more about God. After bible study, her father-in-law asked if anyone desired prayer. As he walked around praying for others, when it was my turn he asked if I had received the Holy Ghost. My reply to him was, "No sir, I have not." Instantly, he began praying for me to be filled. He told me the next time I saw him I would be filled. The following week from Monday to Friday I was nervous for some reason. In my heart I knew it was going to happen, but my mind was all over the place. Saturday finally came, As I was on my way to bible study I noticed something strange taking place in the pit of my belly. Once bible study was over, the minister asked if I was ready to receive the in filling of the Holy Spirt. On the inside, I felt the tug again in the pit of my stomach. He placed his hand on my head. My best friend and her mother-in-law circled around me, and I received the in filling of the Holy Spirit.

The next day, I was sitting on my couch listening to 'Yes' by Shekinah Glory Ministries and my head started to move up and down. Next, my lips began to quiver. I felt something deep down in my stomach moving, Once I opened my mouth, I was speaking in another language. I could not stop myself. I was aware I was not speaking English, but I could not stop it. Before I knew it, I was crying and lifting up my hands. I went to the kitchen, found some oil, prayed over it, and began anointing my house. Hours had passed when I finally stopped speaking in tongues. The best way I can describe receiving the Holy Spirit is awareness.

The Holy Spirit makes you aware of things you would not normally notice. You no longer see things or situations in the natural. When I left my house the next day, everything around me looked brighter as if I was viewing it in high definition. The leaves on the trees looked greener. The sun seemed to shine brighter. It seemed to shine directly on me. The bible says the Holy Spirit does not dwell in an unclean temple. I believe the time I was spending reading my bible was God cleansing my temple.

Reading my bible was even different now. It seemed as if the words leaped off the pages. I recall reading the book of Matthew and stopping to smile as looked up to heaven to tell Jesus, "Lord you did not mix words." He set the Pharisees straight! It was exciting to gaining an understanding of God's Word. As I continued to read the bible, the Lord would place sermons on my heart. I purchased a journal to write my sermons and thoughts down.

Now when I share my testimony with others about the goodness of God. I always make sure I tell them how much love the way God works in my life. When he began to change me, I did not even realize I was undergoing transformation. He used other people to tell me I had changed. I must tell you I absolutely love it. When I look back over my life I was headed for self-destruction, But God. I know for a fact that I, Nicole Re'Nell Dudley, did not change myself. It was God who changed me.

I have found confidence, self-worth, identity, self-esteem, stability, joy, peace, love and many other wonderful things in Christ Jesus! When I was with those men, I always felt something was missing. I never felt complete. I realized what I was missing was a relationship with the Lord.

Whenever I had a question or a thought about something, I would find it while reading my bible, God would direct me to the answer. It was beautiful developing my relationship Him. The more I became rooted and grounded in the word, the easier it was to obey. Things I previously indulged in no longer excited me. Places I once went, I no longer had a desire to go. Each day, God reveals to me this is what He has called me to do. On a daily basis He sends women across my path for me to minister to and encourage. It is such an honor and privilege to be used by God. Without him I can do nothing.

Everything we are comes from the Lord. The air we breathe comes from Him. If it were not for the measure of faith He has given to every man, we would not be able to believe. The bible says who the Son sets free is free indeed. God's word is true. You cannot stay the same when the Lord reveals His truth to you.

I never imagined in a million years I would be here writing about my life and sharing my failures and mistakes with the world. Yet, the Lord told me this is not about me, but my story is about Him. When I give Him all the glory, honor, and praise it encourages other women by letting them know they are not alone. God took this filthy misshapen lump of clay and placed her on the potter's wheel. He still continues to mold, shape, purge, and prune me for His glory. I pray you were encouraged by my testimony. God is truly worthy to be praised!

Chapter Fifteen

Releasing Soul Ties

Soul ties are described as a linkage in the soul realm between two people. It links their souls together, which can bring fourth both positive and negative results. Soul ties formed from sex outside of marriage causes a person to become defiled. When my cousins molested me all those years ago, they left part of themselves with me. Every person I was intimate with after that time I gave them a part of me. I did not just offer up my body, but so much more. I am referring to the part we do not see and in turn do not recognize. This is what we call soul ties.

Prior to now, I never knew why I became attached to every person I had intimate contact with. Once God delivered me, I had to go through a purging process. It was necessary in order to rid myself of all those things which were not of him.

Earlier in the story I mentioned Calvin, the guy who I had an on again off again relationship with. My friends often asked me why I continued to see Calvin when he treated me like a bald-headed stepchild. Honestly, I did not have an answer. I simply shrugged my shoulders.

During those ten years, I could never fully let Calvin completely go because in my mind, I loved him. I mean truly loved him.

I loved a man who never took me out and only saw me at night. He only called me when he wanted to be intimate with me. Yet, I was drawn to him like a moth to a flame. There were times when I could not reach Calvin, I would go into a manic rage. I would call him continuously until he answered. Once he answered the phone I would just cry uncontrollably. It was not until the Lord totally delivered me I learned the true meaning of soul ties.

One day while I was watching a sermon by Bishop T.D. Jakes, he began preaching on soul ties and the sacrifice of praise. Every time I denied my flesh the opportunity to be with Calvin, I became an offering to the Lord as a sacrifice of praise. Truly, there have been times since my deliverance I thought about going back to Calvin. However, I love the Lord more than I love Calvin. Now, each time a thought enters my mind to be with Calvin. I begin telling the Lord how much I love him. I remember how far God has brought me. and in doing so I am offering him sacrifices of praise. With every sound of praise, I release unto the Lord, it breaks a piece of the soul tie. As I continue to give God praise, eventually the soul ties will be removed far from me.

Once you give God a "YES," be prepared to let go of things you hold dear. In 2017, I moved out of my parents' home because there was an urgency for me to leave. I started receiving what I now call spiritual checks. God began revealing things to me about my family I did not agree with. One thing I knew for sure. My time had come to leave my family behind.

The night before I left, my mother came into my room. She told me, "Nicole you need to stop being fake with the people at your church." You cannot go around turning your love on and off. You are not going to finish school. You are not going to make anything of yourself. After she released those words, she turned around and left. The next morning, I secretly packed my things and left. I was determined to never look back.

I stayed in a hotel for two days until my apartment was ready for me to move in. I remember telling God I do not know what is going on, but I trust you. When I let go of the one thing I held dear, God showed up in my apartment. While I was sitting in the corner my purpose was revealed to me. My family was one of my most difficult soul ties to let go. God wanted to release me from the mindset I grew up in.

An entire year passed, and I had no communication with my family. On May 19, 2018 I received a call from my sister that my mother was not breathing. Immediately I jumped up and rushed to their house. Once I arrived the ambulance and police were everywhere. My mother was locked in her bedroom while the EMTs worked to revive her. While everyone around me was crying, I began to pray. I told God nothing He does is a coincidence. No matter what happened, my mother was healed. I believe you will take the sickness from her or you take her from the sickness.

As the EMTs came out of the house with my mother on the stretcher. They headed to the hospital. My family arrived shortly after the ambulance at the emergency room. While we were on our way to the hospital the doctor pronounced my mother dead. I went into a state of confusion. How could God tell me to leave my family, deliver me, and fill me with his Holy Spirit only to take my mother away from me. The enemy tried to get me to doubt God by saying my experiences with Him were not real. Instead of doubting God, I ran to him.

On the day of my mother's homegoing, I danced before her casket. I gave God all the glory, honor, and praise for the life my mother lived. I also praised Him for the time He gave me with my mother. I can honestly say for myself that all things do work together for the good of them that love God and to them that are called according to His purpose.

I have been through the fire. I have seen the lighting flash and I have heard the thunder roar. On the road to my purpose, I've had to let some people go. I cried many nights, but my God said in His word that, "weeping may endure for a night but joy cometh in the morning." Psalms 30:5 (KJV).

Morning has broken, and I am arising into the dawning of a new day.

Chapter Sixteen

Walking in Purpose

The purpose of this book is to serve notice on the enemy. I came to let him, and his demons know we will no longer live with the insecurities, doubts, fears, and mistakes of our past. We will now live as the fearfully and wonderfully made women Christ created us to be. Every plot the enemy used to hold you down is the very thing God will use for His glory.

Growing up, I never understood why I was so emotional. The enemy often told me it was because I was weak. Sorry to disappoint your devil, but when God created me, He looked at me and said I was good. The weakness the enemy wanted me to believe existed in my life, were actually strengths given to me by God. What the enemy called weakness, God called compassion.

The reason the enemy attempts to destroy you is because he sees your future. He knows how good God is because he has seen and experienced God for himself. The enemy also knows God wants good things for His children. Because of how God loves and cares for us, the enemy truly hates us. He wants to keep us from receiving the blessings God has for us.

The enemy knew I would eventually come to Christ. Even as little girl, he did everything he could to prolong me from reaching my purpose. The good news today is, the enemy has no authority to stop God's purpose for your life. Satan is defeated and has no power. The only thing he can do is try to distract you. One thing scares the enemy, it is an unlocked mind. A mind that is set free is not a match for him. Once you are set free, Satan no longer has control over you.

Ladies it is time to take back our minds! The enemy has no authority here. I decree and declare in the name of Jesus you are free. Free from the bondage of your past, free from the bondage of the molestation, free from the bondage of those mistakes, free from the bondage of the no-good man who put you through hell. Never forget you are fearfully and wonderfully made.

I want to encourage you to walk in your purpose. Trials may come. Storms may rise but remember that no weapon formed against you shall prosper.

Take this time to truly reflect over your life. I encourage you to get into a quiet place with no distractions and allow the Holy Spirit to move and minister to you. In the book of Isaiah 53:5 (KJV) he writes, "But he was wounded for our transgressions, he was bruised for our iniquities: the chastisement of our peace was upon him; and with his stripes we are healed. In Jesus name."

Purpose Journal

Purpose was a part of our DNA before we were born. It will always be at the core of who God called us to be. Once you discover your true purpose, you become unstoppable. The process towards purpose can be hard, but true beauty is the end result. Take a moment to reflect over your life. What is one area or areas you have been attacked the most?

____

____

____

____

If you believe God has revealed your purpose to you, I encourage you to write it down here. Include how you believe He led you to it.

____

____

____

____

____

If you are unsure of your God ordained purpose, I encourage you to seek Him in prayer. Also begin daily writing down your words of confirmation He speaks and prophetic words you may receive from others. Periodically take a moment to write Him a love note. God loves to hear from his daughters. Remember "All things work together for the good of them that love God, to them who are called according to his purpose." (Romans 8:28) (KJV)

____

____

____

____

____

Towards the end of my journey to discovering my purpose, I went through a phase. It was difficult to let go of past issues in my life. In order to be used by God you must surrender your **mind**, **body**, and **soul**. If you believe you are on the path to discovering your purpose, it is critical to identify your current phase in the process. Are you surrendering your: Mind, Body, or Soul?

____

____

____

____

____

www.ingramcontent.com/pod-product-compliance
Lightning Source LLC
LaVergne TN
LVHW010107110826
845155LV00028B/534